THE
FLYING
SHOES

BERNICE MYERS

LOTHROP, LEE & SHEPARD BOOKS · NEW YORK

For Olivia with love

First Edition   1   2   3   4   5   6   7   8   9   10

Library of Congress Cataloging in Publication Data
Myers, Bernice. The flying shoes / Bernice Myers.
  p.   cm.   Summary: Dogma Barker sets off to deliver her gift of flying shoes to the queen, but Cattails the sneak thief tries
to steal them from her. ISBN 0-688-10695-1. — ISBN 0-688-10696-X (lib. bdg.)   [1. Shoes—Fiction.   2. Flying machines—
Fiction.   3. Animals—Fiction.]   I. Title. PZ7.M9817Fl   1992   [E]—dc20
91-3354   CIP   AC

Dogma Barker
and her mother
earned their living
by making shoes.
All kinds of shoes
for all kinds of feet.

The trouble was,
they made more shoes
than they were able
to sell.
So the piggy bank
was always half empty.
"Don't worry, Mama,"
said Dogma. "Someday
things will get better."
But they didn't.

One evening
Mrs. Barker was
reading the paper.
"Queen Narr of Glick
is getting married.
She's offering a
Grand Prize for
the most original
wedding present."
"Mama, we can make
her a pair of shoes.
A pair of—of—of
FLYING SHOES!"
shouted Dogma.
"If we win, we'll
be famous."

Dogma was getting
more and more excited.
"People will come from
miles around just to
buy our shoes!
We'll have money for food
and for ballgames
and parties and..."
Dogma's mother listened
to all the wonderful things
they would do as she stitched
the hard leather.
But someone else
was also listening:
Cattails, the thief.

A few days later
the shoes were finished.
"They're perfect, Mama!"
said Dogma.
"Just perfect!"
They decided
Dogma would deliver
the shoes to the Queen.
Mrs. Barker gave her
the little money she had saved.
Then she took Dogma
to the bus stop.

"Now remember,"
said Mrs. Barker.
"Watch out for
that thief, Cattails.
He has many disguises.
Look both ways
before crossing the street.
And above all
don't give the package
to anyone
but the Queen."

Dogma took her seat
on the bus and
held the package
tightly on her lap.
No sooner had the bus left
than a voice behind her
began asking questions.
"What's in the package?
Is it a present?
Can I have it?"
He must be the thief
Mama warned me about,
Dogma thought.
And she held on
to the package
even tighter.

DRAT!

The bus dropped
the passengers
off at the dock
and Dogma
boarded a ship.
The whistle blew
and the ship sailed
out of the harbor

The ocean waves
rocked the ship and
made Dogma seasick.
She went straight to
her cabin and
straight to bed.

She had been sleeping
only a few minutes
when the door
slowly opened.
It was Cattails.
He tiptoed into
the cabin
and reached out
to grab the package.

But before he could
snatch it,
the ship rocked
and Cattails
tumbled backward
out the door…

which slammed shut after him.

A few days later
the ship reached port.
Dogma was the last one off.
A taxi was
waiting for her.

"Here, let me help you
with that package,"
said Cattails.
"It must be very heavy."
"No, thank you,"
said Dogma as she
got into the cab…

...and got out again
when the car wouldn't start.
Dogma got into another taxi,
which drove her to
the train station.

Dogma boarded the train
just in time.
She sat near the window
and looked out.
Suddenly a face appeared.
"Oh, the poor thing,"
said Dogma.
"He must have just
missed the train."

Dogma opened the
window and helped him
climb inside.
"Water, water, water,"
he begged.
"Nurse, nurse, nurse,"
he added.

Dogma ran out
into the passageway.
Cattails reached up
for the package.
"At last!" he cried.
"At last I have
the Flying Shoes!
Here's my chance
to win the big prize!
I'll be rich....
I'll be famous...."
"Tickets. Tickets, please,"
said the conductor.
"Your ticket, sir?"
But Cattails
didn't have one.

When Dogma returned
with the nurse
and some water,
Cattails was gone.
"I guess he felt better,"
Dogma said.

When Dogma got off at
the station in Glick,
she signaled for
transportation.
"Over here, miss."
Dogma looked both ways
before crossing the street.

"To the palace, please,"
she said
and climbed up
on the camel.
My, the camel-driver
looks familiar,
Dogma thought.

"Sit," he shouted
at the camel.
"Sit! Sit!
SIT DOWN!"
And sit it did.

"Up!" shouted the
camel driver.
"UP! GET UP!"
But the camel wouldn't.
Dogma was in a hurry
to get to the palace.

DRAT!

"Please, sir,
don't worry about me.
I'll just walk."

By the time
Cattails freed himself,
Dogma was already
at the palace.
Queen Narr
was opening up
her presents.

Dogma got in line
and waited her turn.
"Please help
a poor old man,"
said a voice
next to her.
"You're not old,"
said Dogma.
"But I will be someday,"
he said.
Feeling sorry for him,
Dogma looked in her
pockets for a coin.
"Here, dear child,"
he said.
"Permit me to hold
your package
while you look."
And Dogma,
forgetting what she had
promised her mother,
gave it to him.

Cattails ran to
the head of the line.
"Your Highness,"
he cried.
"I bring you the world's
first pair of flying shoes.
Shoes fit only for the feet
of a beautiful Queen.
Shoes to fly you
hither and thither!"
And he helped her
put them on.
"Well," said Queen Narr,
"I don't seem to be
flying, do I?
What happens now?"
"Er," said Cattails,
"I don't know."
"You don't know?"
said Queen Narr.
"Er, I don't remember."
"You don't remember!"

"But I remember!"
Dogma shouted out.
And she pushed the
secret button
that sent Queen Narr
skyward.

After circling
the palace twice,
Queen Narr returned
to give Dogma
the Grand Prize:
a parrot.
She gave
Cattails, the thief,
a year in jail.

Dogma returned home
the following day.
Her mother was
happy to see her,
but a little disappointed
in the Grand Prize.
"You brought home
a parrot?
The Grand Prize
was a stupid old
parrot?"
But the Barkers
soon learned
that their parrot
had magical powers.

Dogma and her mother
did become famous.
And everyone did come
from miles around
to buy their shoes.

Even Queen Narr
and her family,
who fly in to visit
every summer.